Little, Brown and Company
Hachette Book Group
1290 Avenue of the Americas, New York, NY 10104
Visit us at LBYR.com
mylittlepony.com

First Edition: May 2018

LB kids is an imprint of Little, Brown and Company.
The LB kids name and logo are trademarks of Hachette Book Group, Inc.

The publisher is not responsible for websites (or their content) that are not owned by the publisher.

Library of Congress Control Number 2017959125

ISBNs: 978-0-316-47551-8 (pbk.), 978-0-316-47556-3 (ebook),
978-0-316-47554-9 (ebook), 978-0-316-47550-1 (ebook)

Printed in the United States of America.

CW

10 9 8 7 6 5 4 3 2 1

Licensed By:

The Perfect Pear

Based on the episode "The Perfect Pear"
by **Joanna Lewis and Kristine Songco**
Adapted by **Louise Alexander**

LITTLE, BROWN & COMPANY
LB kids

One sunny afternoon, Apple Bloom galloped through the market and noticed a new stand.

The kind-looking old pony behind the counter could barely keep up with the crowd lining up to buy his pear jam.

When she got to the front, he nudged a sample across the counter.

Tasting the sweet jam, she smiled. "Welcome to Ponyville! I'm Apple Bloom!"

"I'm Grand Pear. And it's welcome *back*! Decided to move my jam shop home after many years up in Vanhoover."

"Well, I'm glad you and your delicious jam are back," Apple Bloom declared.

"Thanks." He smiled. "Have a jar on the house."

As Apple Bloom waved good-bye, he added, "Come back and visit sometime!"

Back home, Apple Bloom announced, "I got the perfect toppin' for flapjacks!"

The reaction was not what she expected.

A shocked Applejack grabbed the jar and tossed it to Big Mac.

"Woah, what's the big deal with *pear jam*?"
Apple Bloom asked, watching her siblings
scramble to hide the jar.

"The Apples and the Pears are enemies,"
Applejack hissed.

"E'yup." Big Mac nodded.

"But...*why*?"

Big Mac shrugged.

"I, uh…I don't know," Applejack admitted. "Granny gets so upset if I even say 'pear,' I've always been too nervous to ask."

With Grand Pear back in town, it was finally time to find out what had happened between the Apples and the Pears.

Apple Bloom, Applejack, and Big Mac visited Goldie Delicious for a history lesson.

"I have the full story in here somewhere…" Goldie said.

Digging into a giant pile of books, she pulled out one called *Apple Family History Volume 137*.

Years ago, Grand Pear's farm sat next to Granny Smith's. They both took great care of their orchards, but instead of appreciating each other's fruit, they bickered about whose was best.

"Rotten Pear!"
"Sour Apple!"

Apples did not talk to Pears. Pears did not talk to Apples.

But one day, little Bright Mac spotted a friendly filly across the Apple-Pear fence and broke the rules.

"Y'know, if you hold a buttercup under your chin, it'll glow," he whispered.

Lifting up a flower, she grinned. "Does it work?"

He smiled. "It sure does, Buttercup."

Applejack interrupted. "Bright Mac? Buttercup? Those are our parent's names!"

"Oh yes," Goldie remembered. "Buttercup was the nickname your daddy gave your mother. Her given name was *Pear* Butter."

"You're sayin'," Applejack gasped, "OUR MOTHER WAS A...*PEAR*?"
"So we're HALF PEAR?" Big Mac cried.

Goldie nodded. "Even though their families were enemies, your parents' love for each other was magical."

She then sent them to talk to Burnt Oak, Bright Mac's closest friend, for more of the story.

"Yep, we were thick as thieves," Burnt Oak chuckled. "One day, as we were racing in the fields, your dad spotted your ma.

"He was so distracted by the sight of her, he tore through the fence and tipped over the Pear water silo!"

Burnt Oak smiled at the memory. "Your daddy knew he'd be in trouble, but he went up to Grand Pear and confessed to the damage."

"Dad was super honest!" Apple Bloom nudged her sister. "Apple doesn't fall far from the tree, huh, Applejack?"

Bright Mac spent every day fixing up the water silo...
and getting to know Buttercup.

"She was a real peach of a Pear," Burnt Oak finished. "If you wanna know more, I reckon you should talk to Mrs. Cake."

Soon Mrs. Cake gushed about Buttercup as she bustled around her store.

"She convinced me to start baking by bringing me all the ingredients for pear upside-down cake. She knew my calling before I did!"

Applejack turned to Apple Bloom. "Helpin' ponies find their true talents—like you, sugarcube!"

To thank her friend, Mrs. Cake baked a special treat. She was on her way to deliver it when she spotted Buttercup enjoying a picnic with Bright Mac.

"They explained that their families didn't get along, so I promised to keep their secret."

Over the next few months, Buttercup and Bright Mac found ways to see each other in secret.

They'd sneak off to share milk shakes and long walks in all seasons, enjoying every moment they could steal with each other.

On the anniversary of the day they met, Buttercup sang Bright Mac a song:
We're far apart in every way,
But you're the best part of my day,
And sure as I breathe the air,
I know we are the perfect pair.

Things seemed almost perfect. But then Grand Pear announced the Pear family was moving to Vanhoover. It would be good for business, but also, he added, they would get away from those gosh darn Apples....

Buttercup's heart broke. She would be separated from Bright Mac forever.

Bright Mac made a big decision. "I know I never want to be apart from you—ever. I'm so sure, Buttercup, I'd marry you today."

So he proposed!

Of course, Buttercup said yes.

Between pear and apple trees, Buttercup and Bright Mac had a secret wedding under a full moon.

They sealed their bond by planting some seeds. It was a humble ceremony, but it was full of love.

Just as it ended, Granny Smith and Grand Pear stormed into the clearing.

"You two can't be married!" Granny screeched.

"For once, we agree!" Grand Pear shouted. "You've got to stick by your family!"

Buttercup was torn. "But... the Apples are my family now, too," she explained.

"You're choosing to be an Apple...over a Pear?"
Grand Pear growled.

Buttercup gulped. "Yes. I am."

So this was why Granny had never told Big Mac, Applejack, and Apple Bloom the full, sad story of the feud. Now it was time to make amends.

Apple Bloom led the way to Grand Pear and introduced him to her brother and sister.

The old pony burst into tears at the sight of his grandponies, sad he had missed so much time with them.

The Apple siblings embraced him.

Soon, Applejack, Apple Bloom, and Big Mac came back home, where Granny was waiting.

"Where have y'all been hidin'?" she asked.

Applejack stepped forward. "We've been all over, learnin' about our parents. And meetin' our grandfather."

Big Mac stepped aside to reveal Grand Pear.

"Learnin' about Mom and Dad," Apple Bloom reflected, "I found a piece of myself!"

"I feel closer to them," Applejack added.

"I should have told you sooner." Granny hung her head.

Grand Pear sobbed, "I'm sorry I let a silly feud keep me from family."

Applejack spoke up, "Let's not miss any more time together."

"Welcome back, you prickly pear." Granny grinned.

"Thanks, you old crab apple."

At long last, the former enemies shook hooves.

"Now that we're all together, we have somethin' to show you," Apple Bloom announced.

As the family entered a clearing, the grandparents gasped.
"It's beautiful," Granny whispered.
"It's...impossible," Grand Pear marveled.

Before them stood a treasure, planted years ago by Bright Mac and Buttercup.

"If anything's gonna make it," Applejack insisted, "it's family."

"E'yup," Big Mac agreed.

After all these years, the ponies all stood together as one family in front of two magnificent trees—one apple, one pear—twisted together in a heart.